# A NOVEL THIEF

## A WINTER FALLS MYSTERY

### BOOK I

JESSICA BAKER

Celestial Pen Books

Book One of *A Winter Falls Mystery.*



First Edition: October 2023.

ISBN: 978-1-960102-05-8 (paperback)
ISBN: 978-1-960102-04-1 (e-book)

Published 2023 by Celestial Pen Books.

# A NOVEL THIEF
## A WINTER FALLS MYSTERY

# Prologue

THE TYPEWRITER in the apartment above the bookstore belonged to my great-grandfather. Dad and his father never touched it. But when I was little, my great-grandpa would sit me on his knee at the desk and show me how to type. The keyboard needed more pressure than a computer, but it felt so different from just that. There was something magical about the typewriter. Perhaps it was just the romance of it all, like writing with pen and paper.

My dad now owned the bookstore, but the upstairs space was only for me. I spent hours at that typewriter creating stories about butterflies landing on the flowers at the rose garden down the street. About mysterious passengers on the train behind the shop and all the exciting places they were going. About a dark prince coming to sweep me off my feet when the girls at school picked on me for choosing to write stories instead of gawking at the football team.

My dad loved Edgar Allan Poe's *The Raven*. The poem was printed across one of the walls of our family's bookshop for as long as I could remember and framed by painted ravens taking flight. He even wanted to rename the shop "The Raven" after my great-grandpa died, much to my grandpa and my mom's dismay. They wouldn't let him change the shop name, but he had, however, gotten his way when I was born and named me Lenore.

Perhaps it was just a coincidence, but sometimes, it really felt like the stories came true.

# One

THE BOOKSTORE WAS ALWAYS empty this late in the day. A bit later tonight it would come alive with the members of the book club that met every other week after store hours. Mom ran the book club and she was forever trying to get me to join. For the most part, I could find plenty of reasons to hide out in my room above the shop.

I always stayed upstairs during book club nights. While I worked in a bookstore and had been raised in the store, the idea of organized reading seemed painfully boring to me.

I left for college just after high school with the intention of finding grand adventures away from the slow little town. I wished I had actually gone on those adventures. After finishing college, I came home to work in the bookstore. I didn't travel or really go to see anything. In college, studying was my priority and during my breaks, I worked at the campus bookstore. Everything became "someday".

Winter Falls wasn't a bad place to live though. It didn't look like what people generally imagined when they pictured Florida. There were no beaches, few palm trees, and it was cloudy more days than not. It was only about an hour's drive to the beach, a little more to any of the bigger stores. The town was very much idyllic America, almost exactly what you'd expect on a postcard of somewhere more north than here. Orange groves were to the west.

The main streets through town had live oaks that dripped with Spanish moss.

Fall in Florida was almost non-existent. Fall foliage didn't exist in the traditional sense. The leaves would all decide to drop off the tree one day. The hot summer temperatures would shift into hot winter temperatures, only to drop into freezing cold and go right to hot again. I wore a tank top and sandals most of winter, only pulling out a sweater on the rare days like today when there was the slightest chill in the air.

Tonight was no different than the other book club meeting nights, other than I hadn't already gone upstairs by the time the first person came. Mom was running late, so I was still downstairs when the bells chimed and a man walked in.

He was tall and younger than the usual group that joined Mom. I felt like I knew him from somewhere, but he definitely wasn't one of the members of her book club that I had seen before. He looked around the shop before his gaze settled on me and my breath caught in my chest. His eyes were a fathomless abyss that I could have drowned in.

"Is this where Joanne's book club meeting is?"

Even his voice was familiar, like something from a dream.

"Are you part of the group?"

He smiled. "I met Joanne at the coffee shop across the street. She invited me."

"I'm Lenore, Joanne's daughter."

He offered a firm handshake and his grin warmed my insides. "You may call me Sean."

"They usually meet in the back." I motioned to the chairs that I had started setting up on the other end of the store. "It's just a bit early."

"I don't mind waiting."

If Mom had invited him, he couldn't be too bad. She had a sort of intuition about that kind of thing. Somehow, people never disappointed Mom. Even when they weren't what they first appeared to be, she never seemed to face the sort of problems that the rest of us did.

It was awkward trying to finish setting up with Sean's eyes following my every move. I wasn't the biggest fan of being watched, yet with every move I made, I could feel his gaze on me.

"When'd you move to Winter Falls?" It couldn't have been very long. I would have remembered seeing him.

Small talk had never been my strong suit. Hopefully, he would equate my abruptness with friendliness and not be offended.

It was fortunate that Mom rescued me from having to socialize more. The door clanged open, the bells chiming as they hit the door frame, and she stepped inside.

"Sean! How lovely. You were able to make it after all."

He turned to her with that strange, charming smile. "It was very kind of you to invite me."

She turned to me.

"You haven't finished setting up yet?"

I shrugged, unfolding the last chair. Mom sighed, but Sean seemed oddly amused by it. "I'm heading up, unless there's anything else." She was silent so I kissed her cheek. "Have fun!"

THE KEYS WERE familiar beneath my fingers, warm and solid as I pressed each one. The story hadn't been flowing easily the last few days, but I liked to blame the distraction of running the shop and preparing for book club. The pages I had already typed lay in a neat stack on the corner of my desk. The clock necklace my great-grandmother had given me sat around my neck, ticking steadily, echoing every beat of my heart. Once I managed to get a rhythm going, it felt like I finally knew where I was going with it.

The bell dinged when I reached the end of the row and I

pressed the carriage return. The paper slid up, scratching slightly along the back bar meant to keep the paper upright.

*The man wore dark clothing, his face obscured by a mask. Only his eyes were visible, catching the moonlight as he looked around the room.*

*He walked forward slowly, taking care not to hit any squeaky floorboards. He stopped at the nightstand and picked up the portrait on top of it. The man traced his finger over the tarnished locket that hung from her neck.*

*"So greedy," he huffed as he set the miniature down again. "So willing to take what wasn't yours."*

*He pulled the nightstand open and removed a small jewelry box. Inside was the locket from the painting. He plucked it out, glistening in the dim light.*

*The pitter-patter of feet across the floor startled him.*

*"Meow?" The cat stared up at him with bright green eyes.*

The train rumbled as it came through the station, rattling the windows in their frames, and I stopped typing. It would be gone in a few minutes, but the distraction was enough to throw me off. I glanced out the window. Just the usual Amtrak passing by. The station was a historic landmark and the people traveling by train used to bring business to the town. But trains didn't stop in Winter Falls anymore. They hadn't stopped here in a long time.

I always liked watching the trains. As a child, I used to sit on the window seat downstairs and stare out as they passed. As an adult, I found it no less fascinating.

It left as suddenly as it came, chugging slowly past the lake and by the rest of downtown. The red lights on the last car glittered in the lake as the train headed northbound. Someday, I might actually take the train somewhere. It had always been a dream of mine, and one day it would be a reality.

I reached up to my chest and felt for the watch, fiddling with the clasp to open it while I waited. It felt warm in my hands, familiar and comforting in the way it sometimes did.

The noise quieted down for a split second before something creaked behind me. I blinked, trying to adjust my eyes back to the dim light of my office as I scanned the room. Was it just a figment of my imagination or was something really there?

"Hello?"

"Meow?"

The sound came from under my desk. I shoved the chair back and looked underneath. A pair of green eyes peered back at me. A cat? How had a cat gotten in here?

I glanced back at the door. I could have sworn I heard something over there but it was still closed tightly. Perhaps it got in before I came upstairs and had just been sleeping? But how had he gotten in here in the first place? The cat moved out from under my desk, strutted forward, and leaped suddenly onto the typewriter. His paws pressed down the keys and jammed them against the paper and the guide before he settled on my desk, looking very satisfied with himself.

# Two

MY DREAMS THAT NIGHT WERE, for lack of a better description, odd. Every moment felt unusually vivid as I walked through the field. The man I was following was blurry... just an outline against the bright sun and the waves of flowers. With every step came the strangest sense of déjà vu. I'd been here before.

I knew the man too, even though I couldn't see his face or his features. He'd been in my dreams before. He led me through the field, towards a great castle on a cliff overlooking the sea. The sun glimmered in the water, shimmering on the tiny ripples that seemed to make the castle glow with the reflected light. But like everything else, the sun was strange here. It was too soft, too golden, too perfect in how it caught the silver edges of the sapphire sea. The sky looked like a paintbrush had streaked across it, purples and oranges and pinks. A sunset but it always looked that way.

It didn't make sense how I'd know it was always like that though. Everything was familiar, but not.

The flowers made way to a ring of mushrooms, too perfectly even to be natural. My hand reached up to my chest, fingers searching for the watch necklace that should have been there but wasn't. I needed it to go home.

Something shadowed fluttered out of the corner of my eyes and I turned around.

"But don't you want to stay?" a melodious voice whispered on the wind.

A tug on my hand drew me forward, away from the circle.

"Come closer," the voice commanded.

This time when I felt for it, the watch was there. I grasped at it tightly, dove into the circle, and the floor fell out from under my feet.

SLEEP DIDN'T COME EASILY after that. It never did on the nights I had such vivid dreams. Part of me always wanted to go back into them and another part wanted to stay awake, the only sure way to stay away from them.

When it became clear that sleep wouldn't come back, I got up. The apartment was dark save for the nightlights I'd place around so I didn't trip in the dark. The view across the lake in the middle of the night was always eerie, especially when the moonlight reflected across the water. It could have been beautiful, but it was so unlike the ethereal, unnatural place in my dreams that it left me feeling disconcerted instead.

A shadow of something passed by the window and I frowned. A noise creaked in the other room, but it was nothing. I was just imagining things after the weird dream. That had to be it.

I pulled the blanket off the back of the couch and laid down. As I drifted back to sleep, I could see eyes like a void watching me.

THE NEXT MORNING, I went to the coffee shop across from the bookstore, as usual. Mornings were always crowded, despite it being the off-season for the hotel next door. As one of two places that served coffee or breakfast items downtown, there was never a shortage of customers.

Sawyer smiled as he saw me come through the door. We'd known each other forever, like most of the kids who grew up here. Even if we left, there was just something about Winter Falls that drew us back. Probably a lot of people felt like they were drawn back to their childhood homes. It had never been in my plans to come back, but life was funny that way.

Gia Griffin leaned on the counter as she waited for her coffee, eyes towards the door. Her gun and badge were prominently displayed on her dark blue police uniform. In high school, Gia moved here with her parents, and we became friends. But she was skeptical and serious. The idea of pursuing writing seemed like a "fanciful hobby" to her rather than an actual career choice. That never stopped her being the first person to read all the stories I wrote in my high school notebooks instead of the geometry notes I should have been writing down.

"Morning, lovely," Sawyer called out across the counter. "The usual, or you feeling adventurous today?"

"Just coffee, I think."

He scrunched his nose. "Shame."

Sawyer took over managing the coffee shop after high school and had been trying to get me to try whatever "creations" he made. Sometimes, he succeeded in convincing me, but I had never been super adventurous. He turned to get my coffee in a to-go cup and Gia looked back to her phone.

"You're quiet this morning."

Normally, Gia didn't stop talking in the mornings.

Sawyer snorted. "She's been obsessed over the robbery at the McBrides' house last night."

"They were robbed?"

"They were *broken* into," Gia corrected. "As far as anyone can tell, nothing was actually taken. And no one was seen or threatened, so it wasn't a robbery."

"Then why break in?" That didn't make any sense.

Gia let out a sigh. "If I knew, I wouldn't tell you. It's an open investigation until the captain releases that information to the public."

"The McBrides live down the street from my parents." I used to sell candy to them for school fundraisers when I was a kid. Mr. McBride was one of my best customers, though Mrs. McBride had always been a bit snooty.

Sawyer handed Gia her coffee and she took a sip. "I'll be heading back there after this. There's only been the one report. Nothing to worry about." The "yet" went unspoken. "Who's the guy staring at you?"

I glanced back. Sean, the man from the bookstore, watched me from the far side of the cafe. Our eyes met and my breath caught in my throat. I looked away quickly. "I'm not sure. He was at the store last night. Mom invited him."

Gia's brow furrowed. "Want me to see what I can find on him? It won't be much without a name."

"I didn't think you were allowed to use department resources for personal use?"

"He paid with a credit card," Sawyer chimed in helpfully. She glared at him, though Sawyer ignored it as he poked at the tablet. "Sean Ryan. He's bought coffee here the last few days. Cake, too. Has a real sweet tooth."

Sawyer winked at me, and I rolled my eyes.

Gia wrote his name down on a slip of paper before she smiled back at me. "I'm not, but that's what the internet is for."

She put the lid on her coffee and shot me a smile before she headed out the door.

"You know," Sawyer said as he leaned in, "nothing's stopping you from just asking him out."

I groaned. I wasn't sure I could explain it, but it felt like something was stopping me. I wanted to talk to him and ask him why he was suddenly everywhere, why I'd never seen him before last night but I felt like I knew him for a long time, and why no one else found his presence odd. But my tongue felt tied in knots. Instead of walking across the room to him, I took a seat and watched him.

# Three

HAILEY WAS WAITING outside the shop already when I pulled the key out of my pocket. She grinned, bouncing on the balls of her feet. "Morning!"

"Good morning."

Hailey came here most mornings before school. She would be graduating in another month and I planned to steal her time again this summer before she left for college. It would certainly be sad to lose my best customer and employee come fall, but she would be back soon enough.

"Looking for anything specific?"

She shifted her bag on her shoulder. "I finished the second book in that series last night and realized I didn't have book three. Do you have it?"

I closed my eyes. Which book was it that she had been reading?

"The vampire one?"

She shook her head. "The one with the faeries."

I nodded slowly and moved to the Young Adult shelves. The cover art for the faery series had been memorable enough and I knew I'd see the third because the covers had been nearly identical. The title was written in silver foil on the spine and caught the light. Plucking it off the shelf, I held it out to her.

Hailey grinned. "You should read it, Nell. I think you'd really like them."

Nell was definitely my preferred nickname, when people felt the need to shorten my name. Nora never felt right and more than one person had just made up nicknames that they liked with little concern about how I felt about them. I actually liked my name in its entirety, even if I had to tolerate the Edgar Allen Poe jokes that came with it.

"Yeah?"

She nodded. "It reminds me a bit of your story idea."

Hailey was one of the few who had an account at the store, considering she treated the bookstore like it was a library, and the book was added to the list for the month. Hailey grew up here. I used to babysit her when her mom would drop her off before work and when I got older, I used to walk her to school until I left for college.

"Maybe if you finish your story before I leave, you could hold a book release here." She leaned over the counter. "I could plan it. That'd probably look great on my resume."

Hailey planned to go to school for marketing and social media management. When she returned to Winter Falls, she would be a great asset to the shop and help to bring it into this century. There was only so much I could do.

She had a whole host of ideas for updating the website so people could purchase online, as well as bringing in more books from independent authors and promoting them. With all the initiatives to shop with small businesses, making it easier for people to buy from us around the world would be a great way to bring business in. Plus, holding events with local authors would be great for publicity.

And I wanted to be one of those authors. I wanted the Winter Falls Bookstore to be a destination for writers and book enthusiasts alike. Despite living in the age of social media, I never felt more disconnected than when I was on social media. It seemed to come so easily to everyone else and I felt like I was always struggling to keep up with them. People posted so frequently and on so many platforms, but my awkwardness always seemed to come out in videos and trying to keep up with the latest trends.

Hailey never had that issue though, which would make her a perfect addition to the bookstore long term. Assuming she wanted to come back to Winter Falls permanently when she graduated college.

"I'll see you after school."

"Go. You're going to be late."

The bell dinged against the door as she left the shop.

THE GIFT SHOP across the street from the bookstore smelled like incense and candles. Delphia Rogers, the owner, had been my closest friend since elementary school, when we used to play together on the playground. She liked to burn the incense and candles to cleanse the negative energy from the hotel, which was to say that the hotel had tried to buy out the coffee shop and gift store more than once, and it was only the fact that the building that the two were in had been in Delphia's family for a century that saved them.

Despite the front door being wide open, Delphia usually stayed in the back unless there were customers in. Somehow, she always seemed to know.

Beside the gift shop, she used her back room to give psychic readings. It played well with the tourists, especially the newlyweds who wanted to hear that they would have long and happy lives together.

"If you look for answers, you might not like what you find." Delphia said with her back to me.

"Hello to you too." She had always been like this, knowing

things before they were asked. Sometimes, I could almost believe she really was psychic. "Did Gia call you?"

Her head cocked.

I didn't think Gia would actually call her, since the only thing the two of them had in common was me, but she had been known to on occasion, even bringing in Delphia as a psychic on one of her cases a while back. It was one of the rare times I had seen the two of them get along when I wasn't directly involved.

Delphia smiled. "Should she have?"

"There was a break-in last night."

"Was there?"

I rolled my eyes. Sometimes, she took the whole mysterious psychic thing a bit too seriously.

"Was that why you came?"

No. But I wasn't sure why I came into the shop in the first place. The break-in didn't affect me, and yet, something about it felt like it tugged at my mind. The McBrides were by no means the wealthiest people in town. Why break into their house?

"Can you get a read on the thief?"

Delphia smiled and there was something odd about the way she was looking at me. "I think you might have more luck than me."

My breath caught. What did that mean? "Right..." I trailed off.

"You should try the cards."

I frowned, and she motioned to a sealed pack of tarot cards. I picked up the box. It felt heavier than I expected and there was something strange about it. Not that I'd ever let her know that. Delphia would take it as a sign that I was "connecting with the deck" or something like that.

"Right. I'll do that."

I probably would not do that. Trying to figure out how to read them would take a lot of time and, honestly, I didn't believe in most of that anyway. The idea of magic cards that could predict the future was a bit farfetched, even for someone writing a fantasy novel.

"Thanks for these." I waved the pack around in my hand. "I'll buy you a coffee."

Really, I would leave money at the coffee shop and orders for Sawyer to give her whatever fancy coffee she ordered, since Delphia liked stuff like iced caramel macchiatos with extra whip cream and cold brews with extra foam and honey. It would also give her an excuse to actually leave the shop and go flirt with him.

For the life of me, I still didn't know why I went in there in the first place.

THE LITTLE COTTAGE on Grove Drive looked like something out of a fairy tale. With the carefully-controlled ivy sprawling the surrounding fences and trees, it seemed to have grown out of the ground fully formed. The "For Sale" and "For Rent" signs that had been present every time I passed were missing now.

A house as pretty as that didn't deserve to be empty. I hadn't seen any sign of someone moving in though, and with the frequency that I passed by, it would have made sense to see something. No one had mentioned it either and with a town as small as ours, there should have been some gossip about it. Sawyer should have known something.

I watched the house for a while longer. The windows had curtains now. A gnome sat in the front garden. Everything seemed more alive, somehow.

I wanted to go in, to knock on the door and see who answered. Something in my gut said that was a terrible idea. Still, I couldn't help but linger by the fence and watch as the wind swept through

the clovers at the base of the trees. There was something so magical
about it.

I HADN'T BEEN PLANNING to go by the McBrides' house, but
Dad asked if I could bring over his order from the hardware store
after my shift was done. Passing by, the McBride house looked
dark, though that didn't mean much during midday in Florida.
Mrs. McBride was retired, but she always seemed to be lurking. If
it looked like she was never home, she never had to play hospitable
neighbor unless she wanted to.

"Kraa-kraa!"

I jerked around. The biggest crow I'd ever seen sat on the fence
staring at me with oddly familiar eyes. Perhaps it wasn't even a
crow.

"Shoo!"

He cawed again, though it was really more of a croak.

"Lenore Ellis! What on earth are you doing sneaking around in
my rose bushes?"

I jumped. "Mrs. McBride. I heard what happened. I just
wanted to check on how you and Mr. McBride were doing."

She smiled sharply. I was familiar with that look. She thought
we were beneath her. "You might as well come in."

Mrs. McBride pulled iced tea out, pouring two glasses without
ever asking if I wanted any. She had always been *aggressive* in her
hospitality.

The pictures on her wall showed off her prized rose bushes and
her tiny dogs. Oddly, in every photo, she wore a necklace. It was a
plain, silver locket, but it didn't appear to be anything special. But
the truly strange part was that she didn't have it on now.

"What a lovely necklace."

Mrs. McBride walked over to me as her brow tightened in confusion. She looked at the photos and immediately stiffened up. The smile this time was forced. "Thank you." She glanced back at the clock. "It's getting late. Thank you for stopping by to check on us."

She all but shoved me out into the yard, slamming the door shut and I glanced behind me. Perhaps it was just a coincidence but tucked into the wreath on the front door was a gray feather. Most people wouldn't have noticed it or wouldn't have cared, but they hadn't written a thief who left gray feathers as a calling card just last night.

But it had to be a fluke. It couldn't possibly mean anything. Could it?

# Four

WHEN I FIRST MOVED BACK TO Winter Falls, I knew I needed my own space. I couldn't live in my parents' house after being on my own for so long. Even a roommate would be more than I could bear.

As a child, I always admired the beautiful brick apartment buildings near downtown. You could walk to everything nearby, which made for a nice change compared to the rest of Florida where you had to drive everywhere. In college, I felt like I was constantly in the car. The campus was too spread out and there were bears that occasionally made themselves known in the area. If I wanted to go off campus, I had to drive. The bus system wasn't very convenient.

My building was as old as the rest of downtown, making it a historic landmark. It had been designed by the same architect who designed several of the mansions around town. Since the architect was a woman in a time when women rarely held positions of interest, it made the building historically significant, especially to the town. Zella Carroll was born and raised in Winter Falls, the daughter of one of the early settlers here. I always admired her. She did things people said were impossible or not a job for a woman to do. She disappeared when she was young but had been a bright flame in the town's history while she lived.

As a result, my apartment blended the modern style with the art deco that was popular at the time. The stained-glass windows facing the hallway outside of the living room featured tiny colorful birds on orange trees. I lucked out getting a corner apartment on the third floor with a great view of the lake from my bedroom and it had been like a manifestation of my desires that it had actually been in my price range. It was only a one-bedroom apartment, but since I had the space above the bookstore as my own personal office and storage, I didn't need to have a bigger apartment.

I kicked off my shoes at the door.

Gia didn't pick up when I called, but several seconds later, the phone rang again. "Do you know what was stolen from the McBrides'?"

"You know I can't tell you that." I could practically hear the eye roll in her voice.

"Was it a necklace?"

The other end was silent for a long moment. "How did you know that?"

"I may have stopped by and talked to Mrs. McBride."

"Lenore!" Gia snapped.

"She was wearing it in pictures. It was pretty, but definitely not her style. And it didn't look expensive."

Gia sighed. "It wasn't."

"Then why go out of the way to take it?" That was an awful lot of effort to break into a house for only a cheap locket. I didn't really expect Gia to answer that. Any answer would be speculation at best.

"Mrow?"

"What happened?" Gia asked in a panic. I hadn't realized I shrieked.

Sitting in the middle of the floor was the black and white cat from the bookstore last night. Where had he come from? How had he gotten in? The only way would have been if someone let him in, but considering he ran off and disappeared down the stairs last night when I tried to get close to him, I don't even know who would have caught him.

"There's a cat in my apartment."

"What? When did you get a cat?"

"I didn't."

Something rustled on the other end. "I'm coming over."

"What?" I shook my head, grabbed one of my golf clubs from by the front door, and started opening the closet doors with my free hand. There probably wasn't anyone in my house. "Mom must have brought him over. He was wandering around the bookstore during her book club last night."

The laundry room was empty, as was the bathroom. The bedroom and closet were similarly empty and I let out a breath of relief. I didn't think anyone was *actually* here, but there had been that doubt in my mind.

"You still there?"

"Yeah." I set the club back in the bag. "No one's here."

"That's very reassuring."

I rolled my eyes at her dry tone. "I promise I'm fine." The cat had managed to push open my bag and climb into it. He pawed at the binder with my novel, like he was trying to tell me something, and he moved back as soon as I reached for it. With the phone tucked between my shoulder and ear, I set the binder on my coffee table and started flipping through it. "So have you had a chance to look up that guy yet?"

"Sean? Yeah. He just rented that old house on Grove."

"The fairy house?"

I walked past there often. When I moved back, I checked about renting it, but it was well out of my price range. It had been built in the early 1920s and was tucked into a wooded area of land that used to belong to Carroll Mansion, a big historical mansion, before a lot of the land got divided and sold off.

Perhaps it was childish, but I always dreamed of saving up

enough to buy that little house and living there. I memorized every detail I could about the little cottage, stalking it on real estate sites to make sure that if it went up for sale, I'd be the first to know. For as long as I could remember, it had stayed in the same hands. It seemed like some kind of sign that this strange man was living in my dream home after he kept appearing in my life.

"He works for the historical preservation firm and they brought him here. Nothing's really striking me as odd about him." Gia was silent a moment before, "you should ask him out."

"What? No!"

"Why not? If it works out, you can get married and move into your *dream house* and if it doesn't, well, maybe he'll leave town and you can move in there anyway."

"Thank you. I'm hanging up now." She cackled as I hung up the phone. The cat was staring at me. "You really plan on staying with me?"

The cat stretched before lowering his head to his paws. "Meow."

"You need a proper name then." He cocked his head. "And food and... stuff. What do cats even eat? Tuna? You like tuna, right?"

It was official. I had lost my mind. I'm sure that people talked to their pets, but he wasn't my pet. I didn't even know if he was a "he". I didn't know the first thing about having a pet.

The cat blinked up at me. I guess tuna would do.

The date on the can said it was still good, so I opened it up as the cat padded his way into the kitchen. With him occupied, I made my way back to my manuscript and opened it again. Sure enough, the details I wrote about the gray feathers that the thief left were there. But I had forgotten that I wrote the thief as a kind of Robin Hood, only stealing from those who deserved it.

Mrs. McBride must have done something to deserve it, especially to have only a particular locket stolen.

"Kraa-kraa!"

I looked up. On the tree outside the window was the big black bird from earlier.

# Five

THE KNOCK at the door startled me from where I had been staring out the window and watching. The bird outside was freaking me out a bit and I wasn't expecting guests, so I reached for the golf clubs I kept nearby and walked towards the door.

Gia stood in the hallway, still dressed in her uniform. She raised her brows when I didn't move to let her in, shifting slightly to peek around me. "What are you doing here?"

"You screamed on the phone."

I glanced back at the cat, who sat innocently on the ground, licking his paw as if he hadn't tried to give me a heart attack earlier. I moved in and he shuffled out of the way, complaining the entire time. Gia stepped inside and he stopped, staring at her. Maybe her scent was familiar to him.

"Huh," she said, tilting her head ever so slightly. "There really was a cat."

"I know."

The cat preened under our gazes. I suppose I was probably going to need to give him a proper name at one point, but I also didn't plan to keep him.

"You don't happen to want a cat, do you?"

His bright green eyes gave me the most offended glare that a cat could manage. Gia's lips twitched.

I let out a sigh. "Done with your shift?"

She nodded.

"Wine?"

"Please." I pulled out a bottle of wine and set down two glasses. She pulled the holster off her belt and sat it on the counter. "Keep pouring."

I laughed. "Don't you have to drive?"

She laughed. "I walked here. I can walk home."

Fair enough. It wasn't like the police station was so far away. Gia's house was about a mile or so from here. I had done that walk more than once.

When I first came home, Gia offered me her guest bedroom for my use, but her house was tiny, barely bigger than my apartment. Her guest bedroom was about the size of my bathroom now, which was definitely not the sort of place I'd like to live in long term.

The cat huffed and walked towards my room. Somehow, I managed to beat him to the door and closed it before his face. The living room was one thing, but I didn't trust a strange cat with free rein in my bedroom. Who knew if he even had all his shots?

"I guess I'll need the—" I cut off and glanced at the cat. Didn't some animals understand what people said? And this one seemed especially smart. "—V-E-T for him."

Gia took a sip and nodded. "Maybe he's chipped."

"Maybe."

I took my glass and sat down on the couch. Gia walked over and sat down beside me.

"You know, you don't have to live here alone."

I rolled my eyes. "I've lived on my own for years."

To be honest, I wouldn't know bakt to do living with another person. I liked to stay up late writing. I didn't want to disrupt someone else with that kind of schedule. And it would be strange to go from living alone to with someone again. It was bad enough that my mom had a key to my apartment that she frequently made use of. The first few months I came back here, I was sure my apartment was haunted, since she kept coming in and rearranging stuff without saying anything. Somehow, ghost made more sense than family member with a key.

She reached over to the coffee table and picked up one of the loose pages from my binder.

"'The Raven Prince'?" Her brow furrowed. "Why does this sound familiar?"

"It's one of those stories I wrote in high school. You read it."

Not that I expected her or any of my friends to remember every single story I had made them read over the years.

Her phone buzzed and Gia groaned as she checked it. "My mom." She grimaced. "I forgot my aunt and uncle were coming and I'm supposed to be there for dinner. Ugh." She drained the rest of her glass and stood. "I need to get changed. The last time I showed up in uniform while my aunt was there, she made this comment about the reason I'm not married is cause I 'intimidate all the men with my career'."

The cat hissed.

"Exactly," she agreed. "I mean, I'm not even *thirty* yet. It's not like I'm some old maid. But she acts like all my prospects are gone."

In a town this size, prospects was an interesting choice of words. Most of the guys our age were taken or had left town altogether. This wasn't exactly a budding center of commerce. It wasn't like there were nightclubs every block or anything. It said a lot about a town when the bookstore was the center of the community.

The cat made a sympathetic noise and rubbed against her leg. She stooped down and picked him up.

"Maybe I should take you with me. I would love to see the look on my aunt's face if she saw you."

He purred loudly as Gia scratched behind his ears.

"You should take him."

He hissed at me.

"I don't think he likes that idea."

I laughed. "He's got an awful lot of opinions for someone who doesn't pay rent."

He let out a weird noise.

Gia sighed. "I better go." She smiled. "Thanks for the wine."

"Anytime."

MY NEW ROOMMATE chattered the entire time I made dinner. He had opinions on everything. If I didn't add enough spices or herbs, he'd meow loudly to let me know. Too much and he would start hissing. Considering how long I had lived alone, it was extremely frustrating to have someone else making their opinion known so much.

I set dinner on the floor on a plate that I really didn't care about. It took quite a few internet searches to check what exactly a cat could eat, but I was confident that the chicken was perfectly safe. The next thing would be finding a vet that could check if he had owners.

"What am I going to do with you?" I asked him as he curled up on the pillow beside me like he owned the place.

He looked up at me with those eerie green eyes and tilted his head. "Mrow?"

"Yeah, that's what I thought."

I sighed and ran a hand over his head before I turned back to the laptop and typed in "Vets, Winter Falls."

# Six



"HE'S SO SWEET," Hailey cooed as she cuddled the cat. Of course he loved her. He was a talented little actor, charming his way into everyone's hearts, except me. He seemed more than content to boss me around without the slightest care of my opinion.

I brought him with me to the store that morning with the intention to put him upstairs. He shouldn't cause too much trouble there and I had booked an appointment with the vet. It had been a hassle trying to get him out of the house this morning, and I wound up borrowing a cat carrier from Mrs. Tyler next door. My neighbor offered to keep an eye on him, but since I didn't know if he had his shots and all, I didn't want to risk him giving something to her cats, or her cats giving something to him. Better to keep him upstairs where he would be nearby, but away from the customers.

"I didn't know you had a cat. What's his name?"

"I haven't named him yet." He glared at me. "I only found him last night."

Hailey pouted. "I'm sorry."

She kissed his head and he preened.

"I have to go to school," she told him and he pouted, or at least it looked like he was pouting. Did cats pout? "I'll be back later though and see you then. Be good for Nell."

It felt like it sealed my fate that he would be anything but good.

THE VET'S office was noisy and more crowded than I expected. It seemed like everyone in Winter Falls brought their pets in for a check up today.

I sat with the pet carrier at my feet. It felt awkward forcing him in there, but I didn't trust him not to run away and make me chase him. He meowed innocently at me.

"Lenore?"

I looked up. Mr. Roberts led his dog on a leash. The dog sat so politely, staring up at me with those big brown eyes.

"I didn't know you had a pet."

The cat made his presence known loudly, banging against the door with both paws and hissing. The dog even looked taken aback by the racket, eyes growing impossibly wide.

"Oh my."

"I found him the other day."

"Well, good luck to you."

He edged back and his dog followed quickly.

"Why did you do that?" I asked the cat.

He calmed down immediately, and if I didn't know better, I could have sworn the cat was smirking.

"If you're not careful, you might get stuck with a name like 'Demon'."

He glared, but otherwise kept quiet.

"You're right. That's terrible name."

"IT'S SO unlike you to get a pet," my mom said as she came into the shop that afternoon. "I heard from Mr. Roberts that he saw you at the vet this morning."

I groaned. The cat was safely upstairs, roaming to his heart's content. No chip had been found, and he had hissed wildly when the vet tried to give him his shots. As soon as I let him out, he had run under a table and glared when I got too close. The vet asked if I was sending the cat to the shelter, but that seemed cruel when I knew my apartment was pet-friendly. All it would take was a change in paperwork.

"I thought you brought him," I admitted.

"You couldn't remember to feed the goldfish we got you in fourth grade."

I winced. My mom had fed the fish for me for a month before she got annoyed and gave it to my cousin instead. To be fair, I never actually wanted the goldfish. I wanted a turtle and a snake and a dog and a fox. All the fish did was swim around all day and it hadn't been the least bit interesting to watch, especially not for a nine year old with a short attention span and a disposition for fantasy books. The characters in the books always had interesting pets, not a fish.

But I didn't say that. Instead, I shrugged. "Cats mostly take care of themselves, right? And I'm sure Mrs. Tyler would be more than happy to help me out."

She had offered as much this morning, and I fully intended to take her up on that offer. Especially since I didn't know the first thing about taking care of a cat other than what the vet told me this morning.

"If it's your pet, you should be taking care of it."

I didn't want to tell her that it was weird to think of the cat as a mere pet. He seemed too intelligent, too independent, and oddly human. A creature like that could hardly be called a pet.

"And I will. I took him to the vet, didn't I?"

Though I was sure there was more to it than that, it was definitely a good start. And it wasn't like I wasn't surrounded by books and didn't have the internet. It would be easy enough to find out the information I needed to take care of him.

"Lenore..."

I let out a breath. My mom rarely called me by my full name. Usually it signaled that she was annoyed with me or angry or I had done something wrong. She called me 'Nell' because she thought that Lenore was an old name and Nora was even worse. I was rather fond of it though. I didn't mind Nell, but there was something so gothic about the name Lenore that I felt an urge to wear a dark velvet cloak and twirl around in the halls of Carroll Mansion.

If I was being honest with myself, a cat fit that vibe so perfectly, especially living in my probably-haunted century old apartment. All I was missing was a vampire or werewolf or two.

From the look on her face, she could tell what I was thinking.

I could tell she was annoyed with me from how she slammed the door as she left the shop. But it was too late anyway. I was committed, which meant I'd need to succeed at doing this just to spite her.

# Seven

THE BELL tinkled as the door opened and I looked up from the computer. Sean Ryan walked in with two cups of coffee in his hand. He held out one of the take out cups to me and smiled. "Your friend sent me with this."

Across the street, Sawyer stood on the sidewalk. He grinned and threw his thumbs up.

"Thank you."

I winced as the words came out sounding more like a question.

My phone buzzed a moment later and I glanced towards the counter.

"Were you looking for something or...?" My voice trailed off and I realized I had no idea where I was going with that sentence.

He smiled. "I'll browse for a bit, if that's alright with you. See if anything jumps out at me."

His voice had a bit of an accent to it that I hadn't noticed yesterday. I didn't know where he came from and that hadn't been a part of Gia's report on him.

"Of course."

I set the coffee on the counter and watched as Sean wandered between the shelves, scanning the titles as he went.

The text on my phone was from Sawyer.

> He's interested in you. Was asking questions
> earlier.

I ROLLED MY EYES. Of course, Sawyer would take someone asking questions as interest. I took a sniff at the opening of the cup. Smelled sweet and I could see milk. It figured that Sawyer would try to make me be adventurous with my drink when I wasn't there to argue with him.

> What did he ask?

> ...

THE DOTS DISAPPEARED after a few moments, then reappeared again. Sean approached the counter and I hastily locked my phone and flipped it over. It would best if he didn't see whatever it was Sawyer wrote.

Unless, of course, Sean was a serial killer or something. Then I definitely wanted to know that immediately. But if that was the case, would he have really sent him over with a latte.

Sean set several books on the counter, most of them on local history and things to do. Not entirely surprising considering he was new here. But what was surprising was there wasn't a single fictional title among the books he picked up.

"Not a big fiction reader?"

He shrugged. "I suppose not."

Who didn't like fiction? Maybe he was a serial killer after all. It wouldn't surprise me and it would be exactly in line with the other people my friends had tried to set me up with.

"I'm not opposed to it. Just rarely find something I want to read."

I smiled at him. "Well, then you'll have to come back. I'm sure I can find something."

Internally, I cringed. That sounded like I was trying to flirt with him, which was what Sawyer and Gia both seemed to want, but I had only just met him. It seemed weird. Or maybe it didn't sound that way and I was just overthinking it.

Either way, Sean returned the smile. "I look forward to it."

DINNER THAT NIGHT would be takeout, because I had zero interest in cooking when I wanted to be writing. Once again, I opened the binder up and sat down on the couch to begin rereading everything I'd written the last few days. While I know you're not supposed to edit when you're drafting, but something about marking everything up in red was rather soothing.

The cat rather objected to takeout though. Instead, he sat staring until I got up. He led me into the kitchen and pawed at the refrigerator.

"I'm sorry, your majesty," I muttered sarcastically as I pulled out the leftover chicken from yesterday.

He sat proudly, looking more like a puffed up peacock than a cat. With the plate before him, you'd have thought he was a king and I was a lowly servant. It made as much sense as anything else the last few days.

"If that's all."

I walked back to the living room and left him to his dinner. I picked the binder back up again and took a bite of my food. Perhaps the cat had been onto something with wanting the chicken from yesterday instead. But I'd never admit that and let him know he was right.

The new tarot set sat unopened on the coffee table. Delphia said I'd find it useful, but I hadn't. I didn't even know what to do with it. She used to read cards for me at the lunch table in high school, but she once saw something she didn't like and refused to read them ever again. I had asked but she never told me what exactly she saw.

I opened the box.

"Kraa-kraa!"

I jumped and the deck fell out of the box and onto the table. Only one card landed upright. A young man with a sack on his shoulders stood on a cliff. The bottom of the card said "The Fool".

"Kraa-kraa!"

Where was that coming from? For the past few days, it seemed like everywhere in this town was overrun with birds. They were always overhead, always watching in the windows, even invading my dreams.

The sound came again and again and I wanted to clutch my ears and bury my head in my hands. Closing the curtains would do nothing, not when the noise seemed to be coming from everywhere and nowhere all at once.

It stopped then and I looked up.

And there, outside the window once more, was the big black bird.

#  Eight

THE CAT HISSED out the window, his teeth bared and eyes practically glowing. The bird cried out again, but the cat stood his ground. There was something weird about that bird, something wrong about it.

Despite knowing it was stupid, something drew me to the window. Something made me want to open it and walk away. The bird flew in and perched on my coffee table. How did a bird look... *indignant*?

"I know you've been following me." I looked at the bird—was it even a crow?—with the braveness I didn't, in fact, feel. After all, I was talking to a bird. First a cat, now a bird. "What do you want?"

The last thing I expected was for him to hop to the floor and him to transform into a human. If he had been an unfamiliar person to me, I think it would have been less surprising than seeing Sean Ryan standing in the middle of my living room.

I had to be losing my mind. Humans didn't turn into birds and birds didn't turn into men. My mind had to be playing tricks on me. It had to be.

"How did you get in here?"

His forehead creased in amusement, a smirk playing on his lips. "You let me in."

"But..." There was no other explanation. I was going mad. I

had to be. "But that was a bird. You were a bird? How were you a bird?"

"A raven, actually."

"That doesn't even make any sense."

I backed against the wall, reaching for the golf club again, even as Sean sat down on my couch. The cat held his ground, hissing, but seemingly afraid to move closer. I couldn't blame him. I didn't want Sean closer either. "What do you want?"

He chuckled. "You are a rather terrible host, Lenore."

I shuddered. Something about the way he said my name...

"This is my house. I didn't invite you."

Despite that, he leaned back, seemingly unfazed. I contemplated calling Gia, but my phone was on the coffee table by his leg and I didn't think I could get to it before him. I could try running to the door. He might get there before me and block the exit or he might not. It was hard to say.

"But you did."

I frowned and crossed my arms over my chest. I didn't like having defensive body language. It felt like it was too easy to read my thoughts when I did that. I didn't want to let people know when they made me feel uncomfortable, but I needed that physical barrier between him and me. A chair would have been nice. A door would have been better.

"I never met you before the other day. When would I have invited you in?"

"Something drew me to this town many years ago, something that wouldn't let me leave. I thought I found the source of that power at the coven that meets at your bookstore—"

"Coven?" What coven? A coven of what?

"—but it wasn't them." He frowned. "You didn't know?"

"Know what?"

"That your mother is a witch?"

"Excuse me?!"

I knew he had no manners, but there was no reason for him to call my mother names.

"She and her coven meet at your bookstore. To practice their magic," he clarified as he took in my expression. "Did you really not know?"

"My mom was an accountant. She made brownies for my PTA bake sales at school."

He blinked and cocked his head slightly, resembling the bird he had been a short time ago. "What does one have to do with the other?"

I waved my hand around as if that would explain anything. The words wouldn't come easily, or at all really. It was too absurd. The whole thing was absurd. There was no way my mother of all people, my mother who didn't like celebrating Halloween because it was "too spooky" and went to church every Sunday, was a witch. If witches even existed.

Why was I listening to him anyway? There was absolutely no reason to trust him. He was making it all up. Or worse, he actually believed what he was saying.

"Well, then." He sighed. "It doesn't matter anyway. They weren't the source of the spell that trapped me here."

I mouthed the words and they felt as utterly ridiculous on my lips as they did when he said them aloud. "Trapped you where?"

"In Winter Falls," he said as if this should have been painfully obvious.

"I've never seen you before."

His lips quirked. "I've been here. I tried to stay away, tried to return home. But I felt the energy again... the same power that brought me here... it was active and alive last night." He shook his head. "It's hard to explain."

"You sense... *magic?*"

Magic wasn't real. Magic was something I wrote about in my stories and had pretended with my friends when I was little and we'd play magic fairies. But I was old enough to know reality from make-believe and magic was most certainly not real.

He tilted his head. "I suppose that's one way to put it." He smiled. It was a rather pleasant smile, but at the moment, I wanted to punch him in his smug face. "You think it's ludicrous, don't you?"

That felt like a trap. You couldn't tell someone that you thought they were just making up every word that came out of their mouth. "I... I don't know."

He held his hand open towards me, palm facing upwards. And then, it glowed soft white light. I blinked. My eyes had to be playing tricks on me. They had to be. There was no way it was real.

Like a moth to the flame, I stepped forward. He took my hand with his free one, guiding me so that I was the one cupping the light. It felt strange and oddly familiar. The glow from the light was warm, but it didn't burn me.

Magic was *real*?

His smile seemed more genuine this time as if he knew what I was thinking. Perhaps he did. It just all seemed so impossible.

I pulled my hand away and sat down on the couch beside him. "So magic is real and my mom is a witch with a *coven*" —the word sat unfamiliarly in my mouth— "that meets in my dad's bookstore." He stared at me. "So what does that make you? A witch... or whatever a male witch is called?"

Sean chuckled. "A warlock. A male who is born into magic is called a warlock." He shook his head. "But no. Your people call my kind 'faeries'."

If the myths I read about the fae were correct, the comment on hospitality made sense now. The cat meowed loudly on the floor as if to remind us of his presence. It seemed that the cat could sense that I was no longer panicking about Sean being in my apartment. What could I do against someone with actual magic that wasn't even human?

Sean smiled, kneeling to offer his hand to the cat who sniffed at it curiously, then hissed again and pulled away. Sean sat back and studied the cat for a moment.

Why had he even come here to me? What did he hope to gain by telling me any of that?

The bookstore... the energy surge during the meeting... that cat had appeared out of nowhere during the meeting. And Sean... he was here because I had somehow trapped him in Winter Falls. But it was impossible. I didn't even know *how* to do anything.

"I can't help you."

He frowned as he looked away from the cat. "You mean you won't help me?"

I shook my head. "I mean 'can't'. Before a few minutes ago, I didn't even know magic was real. It's just something we pretended was as kids."

He glanced at the table where the deck of tarot cards lay scattered.

"Really?" He sounded skeptical.

"My friend gave them to me."

He plucked the face up card, the Fool, and twirled it in his fingers. "So you don't know what it means?"

I didn't, but now I planned to look it up as soon as I could, if only so I didn't feel like I was missing out on part of the conversation.

He leaned in ever so slightly, keeping his eyes locked on mine. "It means you shouldn't be afraid of a new adventure. How would you have drawn it if you didn't have magic?"

"I *didn't*." I took a breath and tried to keep the hysterical note from my voice. "I dropped the pack and that fell out."

Sean tilted his head again, then stood. "That's okay. We can figure it out."

# Nine

WHEN I WAS A KID, the idea of having magic would have been a dream come true. But knowing it was actually real was another story. How could I help Sean when I didn't have the faintest idea what to do?

My mother apparently had magic for years and lied to me. Did Dad have magic too?

"Did you hear about the break-in at the McBrides' house?" He tilted his head, the motion looking oddly like a bird. "I think I brought the thief here too. Somehow."

It sounded absurd still, even with the thought of magic being real. Did I actually have magic? Maybe that was what Delphia saw all those years ago and why she refused to read any more of my futures. Maybe she knew I wouldn't want to know. Not then, anyway. If she had told me in high school magic was real, I would have assumed it was an elaborate prank, no matter how much I desperately would have wished for it to be otherwise.

The cat jumped up on the couch and laid his head on my leg. I mindlessly stroked his ears and he purred. I nodded my head towards the cat and Sean followed my eyes. "I think I brought him here too. I was writing about the thief getting caught by a cat—"

"Writing?

My manuscript sat open in its binder on the table and it only took me a few moments to flip to the right page before I handed it back to him. Sean took it and read the scene. His fingers traced the letters and a frown overtook his face.

"This hasn't been printed."

I shook my head. "I find it easier to write on my typewriter. And then I can just scan it in."

He flipped the page, reading the scene under his breath as he went.

"You never write anywhere else?"

"I mean, yeah, but the words just flow easier on that than they do when I'm using the computer or writing in long-hand. Something about writing on it just flows so easily." I shook my head. "I can't really explain it."

He cocked his head.

"And the cat appeared as you wrote it?" I nodded. "Hmm." He traced his finger down the page. "Can I see the typewriter?"

"It's not here. It's—"

"—in the shop?"

I sucked in a breath, and he smiled.

"Good news: you might not have magic after all."

He stood.

"And the bad news?"

He smiled. "We need to find this thief so you can put him back in your manuscript."

Sean headed for the door and I scrambled after him, shoving the binder into my bag as I went.

"Wait! *Back* in the manuscript? How would I even do that?"

"How are we even going to track Eirene down?" Sean glanced back at me. The question on his face was as clear as day. "The thief. Her name is Eirene."

Sean frowned. "The story said 'he'?"

"It was a plot twist. The protagonist Amphelisia was watching from the wardrobe and thought the thief was a man, but it turns out it's actually her sister Eirene stealing to help their neighbors. Eirene's been dressing as their brother when she breaks in. He went missing during the war." I grinned. "Did you know that 'Amphelisia' was a common name in the Tudor era, but its origins are not documented? At least, not anywhere that I could find. It just kind of appeared. And then disappeared."

His brow furrowed and he nodded sharply but continued walking. I let out a sigh. Most people asked more when I said I was writing a book. They wanted to know what it was about and always asked for details I wasn't willing to give. But he seemed like he didn't care.

"Have you really been in Winter Falls for over ten years?"

Sean shrugged. "It's easy enough to hide when no one knows to look for you."

His lips quirked up and his eyes grew alight.

I frowned. "But no one's ever seen you. It's a small town. Wouldn't we have seen each other at some point?"

Winter Falls was small. I would have remembered seeing him before. His eyes alone were mesmerizing.

He let out an almost angry sounding breath. "People don't remember me if I don't want them to."

I understood, somehow. In stories, the fae had the power to change people's minds, to make them see things that weren't there. There was another power they had in the stories too, over humans who gave them their name, and I had given him mine.

The sun painted the sky a thousand colors in one of the beautiful sunsets that reminded me of why I loved living here. Brilliant streaks of orange and pink against a still blue background. If we weren't walking so briskly, one might have called the walk romantic. As it was, with his long legs and even longer stride, trying to keep up with him was challenging.

"Hey! What's the rush?"

He hesitated but didn't stop. "It's easier to undo a spell within seventy-two hours of it being cast. We need to find Eirene... and bring her back to the shop before the spell is set permanently." He let out a breath. "And I'll need to examine the typewriter before that, since it seems most likely that it was the typewriter that used the actual spell and not you."

I couldn't begin to explain why I was so disappointed about not having magic. I should have been thrilled. A magic typewriter! An adventure! It sounded like it should have belonged in my book.

But my whole life, I had dreamed about having magic. I made up spells and waved the wand my great-grandma made for my Halloween costume one year, and sometimes, it even felt like the spells worked. But his words hurt, for a reason I didn't want to think too much on. There were people who were special, and no matter how much I wanted to be, I wasn't one of them.

"Where are we going anyway?"

"We need a witch to locate Eirene."

Dread settled in my stomach. If my mom was in fact a witch, she had been lying to me my whole life. If she wasn't, Sean was just making things up and magic wasn't real and he wasn't actually a fae. I wasn't sure which option I really preferred.

"How would a witch locate her?"

Sean shook his head as if he couldn't believe I was actually asking such a question. I *made up* magic in my stories. I didn't know what rules it might abide by in the real world. Who knew what it would actually be like?

A glint of something caught my eye and I reached out, grabbing his arm as I slowed my steps.

"I don't think we need one anyway. Look."

She looked just as I described her earlier in my book, which in our little town, looked pretty far from normal. She might have looked less out of place in Williamsburg or Salem, with the black doublet, hose, and breeches, and I hoped anyone seeing her thought she was wearing shorts and a jacket or cosplaying or something. Anything was better than the truth.

"What—?" He stopped and followed my gaze. "That's her? What is she wearing?"

I rolled my eyes. I liked the late-Tudor era and all the history surrounding it. The class trips we took to St. Augustine were always very cool and the buildings there had sparked my imagination for as long as I could remember. But I also probably could have fleshed out my idea a bit more fully and written a proper outline instead of just writing whatever came to mind as I went. For a first draft, I didn't think the story was bad, but it was definitely a bit convoluted. It would be a long time before it was revised enough that I'd consider letting anyone read the story in full. Between the whole Tudor-era time period, the thief storyline, and the fantasy elements that I barely touched on, it was more of a world-building draft than anything that resembled an actual novel. After this whole experience, I'd definitely be revising it. Heavily. That was if I didn't just scrap the whole thing and start something else instead.

Eirene didn't see us, not at first. When she did, she turned and darted down the street, surprisingly nimble in such awkward clothing.

Sean glanced at me, but I let go of his arm and ran after her. She had a head start, but I had the advantage of actually knowing where I was going. Eirene's footsteps paused as she reached the shoreline. The lake wasn't something I would ever want to swim in, especially thinking about the gators I had seen in it as a kid. It was fortunate that Eirene didn't know how to swim.

"What do you want?" she cried out in her thick accent that matched the one I had made up in my head when I wrote the story.

Sean caught up to us, breathing heavy, which was surprising for someone who claimed they were a supernatural being.

"I want to send you back." Not that I knew how. I hoped he knew or that the answer would become clear once we got her back to the shop. I held out my hand. "If you'll come with us."

# Ten

It wasn't too far of a walk to the shop, thankfully, so we were able to make it back before the sun set completely. Being a weeknight during the off-season, the usual crowds of Lakeview Drive were absent. It was a small relief since I wouldn't have to try to explain to anyone I knew why I was with a man I only just met, escorting a girl who looked like she was cosplaying for a Renaissance faire. Gia would have wanted answers and Sawyer would have interrogated me to no end. It would have fulfilled his ever-present need for gossip for at least a week.

"You can really send me back?" Eirene asked, her eyes wide. I nodded and she let out a sigh of relief. "This place is so strange. It's not anything like I've seen before."

"I know."

She frowned. "Do you?"

I nodded. "I created your world."

She stared at me, but Sean snorted. "That's unlikely."

Like before, his words stung.

"I wrote it."

"No one truly creates worlds. Some people in this realm are just fairly adept at seeing into others. Usually, they become artists of some sort, but Eirene came from another realm, just as I did."

She smiled, her shoulders relaxing. "It relieves me to hear you say so. The thought of everything I've known merely being conceived on the whim of another frightens me greatly."

It didn't provide *me* with any relief, only more questions. After all, who was to say I hadn't pulled other people and creatures into our world from whatever stories I had written on that typewriter? A typewriter that I would be locking away as soon as I figured out how to send Eirene and Sean back.

Though... perhaps it wasn't just the typewriter doing it. After all, if it had been, why hadn't everything I wrote on it come true? Why couldn't anyone write on the typewriter and bring people through?

Did grandpa know when he gave it to me?

"So I have to know. How did you wind up stealing from Mrs. McBride?"

Eirene's brow wrinkled, a frown overtaking her face. "McBride?" Realization struck her. "The necklace?" I nodded. "I... I don't know. I just knew she had taken it from her friend when they were young, so I wanted to give it back. I've always known these kinds of things about people."

"Always?" Despite Sean showing me his magical glowing hands earlier, being a magical repo agent seemed a bit further than I was willing to believe at the moment. That definitely wasn't in my manuscript, although it had definitely been more focused on her sister. Perhaps she really was more than just the character I had written.

I led them through the shop to my upstairs room but hung back near the door as Eirene entered first and then Sean. Part of me bristled at the fact that he treated Eirene with a modicum of respect, but he had barged into my home and dragged me around town without allowing me time to digest his explanation or even fully understand it.

Part of me couldn't help but wonder if he blamed me for his predicament. That was when his attitude towards me changed and became colder. It wasn't my fault that I didn't know how to undo it. I hadn't even known I was doing anything that needed to be undone in the first place.

"I don't know what to do," I hissed at him as he passed by. I didn't want Eirene to hear and lose hope, but I also didn't want to give her any more false hope.

He pursed his lips and moved towards the desk. His hands hovered over the typewriter, frowning. He paused and touched it. A string of colorful curses flew from his lips as he yanked his hands back.

"Where did you get this?"

"What?"

Even if the thing was somehow cursed, I still felt strangely protective of it. It was one of the few things I had from my great-grandpa and I was reluctant to give it up, much less let someone damage it.

He sighed. "It was made by my people. Someone clever, too. It's been tied to some parameter, so only certain people can touch it."

His words gave me a tiny bit of hope. Perhaps I was special after all. Not the kind of special I always dreamed about as a kid, but something that made me different. Unique.

"I don't think anyone else but you will be able to use it."

Eirene glanced curiously between us before her eyes trailed back toward the window where the sun was disappearing beyond the trees on the other side of Little Turtle Lake.

"Right. Okay. How do I do this?"

Sean pulled out the chair, his hand lingering on the edge of the back. "You need to finish the story."

"Finish the—do you know how long that'll take?" I had been stuck for months and if it hadn't been for the bit of inspiration that hit me last night, I never would have made any progress.

"Surely that cannot be the only way?" Eirene asked.

"There's always another way," he said, running his fingers through his hair. "However, such knowledge hadn't been relevant to me." He shot me a quick, unreadable look. "I always assumed that the one that worked the spell to bring me here would know how to undo it."

"I can try, but I don't know if it'll work."

I took a seat and felt his hands shift behind me as he gripped the back of the chair. Though he didn't touch me, his presence was overwhelming. Something so inhuman that it became hard to breathe.

"Magic is all about intent and willpower. You have to want it. You have to believe it'll work."

His frustration was gone in that moment. His voice came softer, melodious, and I could have fallen under his spell so easily.

I closed my eyes. Trying to write with an audience was difficult, but I had been the one to cause this mess. I would be the one to fix it. Despite what Sean said, this was my story. I was its author, its creator, and I could make it go any way I wanted.

I could have used the clock then. The gentle lull of the ticking would have drawn me under into that in-between where time didn't exist. The world would move around me like slow, sweet honey.

The words began to flow after a moment and I let my fingers be guided by whatever strange magic was contained within the keys. My soul already knew where the story would go, it was just my mind that was the block between the story and the page.

I finished the scene and quickly tapped out "The End" before opening my eyes once more. Eirene stared back at me.

# Eleven

I WASN'T sure I would be able to properly describe the disappointment I felt as I saw her. Judging from her expression, Eirene felt the same, not that I could blame her.

The sun would still be hovering just below the tree line. We still had some time. The train had been passing yesterday, but the northbound train didn't usually pass until eight-thirty or so. The cat appeared after the train came by. We had time—not a lot of time, but some time—to figure this out.

My great-grandmother had a watch necklace that I had inherited. It was a strange clock that didn't show 12 hours like most clocks did, but it was always accurate. I loved that necklace and before she died, she placed it around my neck. The world felt strange after that. Time moved faster when I wore it, it felt like. My parents told me it was just puberty. I should have realized it wasn't.

I had been wearing it last night when I brought Eirene and the cat though. If I was correct on when I opened the portal for Sean, I was wearing it then too.

The clock was an ornate, tiny thing, with leaves and flowers and butterflies. Some days, I felt more drawn to it than others. If I was to bet, I'd say that the magic in the typewriter was connected to it somehow.

There wasn't time to go back to my apartment and get it to test that theory. Maybe I could try it some other time.

I tried to summon their image in my head. They were hazy after all these years. The feelings never faded.

She had known though. When grandpa used to bring me up to the typewriter, she used to join us. Her hands would settle on my shoulders as I typed. Things seemed magical then.

I wanted to groan now. They had seemed magical because they *were* magical. Had my great-grandmother been a witch too? My great-grandpa certainly knew, but did Grandpa? Did Dad?

I stood and turned around.

"Maybe there's something around here that might help us."

Sean's brow furrowed as he frowned. "Why would there be?"

I gestured to the rest of the office. "This was originally my great-grandfather's apartment. When he came back from the war, he lived here with my great-grandmother."

My office was their living room before they built their house. Since he had brought the typewriter back with him from Europe, it seemed likely that someone over there had given it to him or he had bought it over there. With any luck, he kept instructions for it here, somewhere that would be easy enough to find.

Sean stared at me, cocking his head.

"What does that have to do with the typewriter?"

I could have smacked myself. "It was his. He's the one who gave it to me. He had to have left something about it here. Somewhere. Maybe?"

It was worth a shot anyway. I wished I could just ask him. There were so many things that I wondered about. Did he know that the typewriter was magical? Had he known when he gave it to me?

It didn't matter now. There was nothing I could do to change the past and I could only work to fix this for Eirene.

Most of the furniture from when it was my great-grandparents' apartment was long gone from the bookstore. It found its way into other family members' homes as heirlooms, or sold to buy pieces more suited to their tastes. I had one of their cabinets as a nightstand in my apartment. Did I have enough time to go back there and look inside? Maybe I had missed something in all the times I cleaned it.

But no. That wasn't grandpa's way. He liked things to be simple. Simple would be to keep the instructions nearby. When I took over the space, I bought a new desk. But Grandpa's original desk on which the typewriter had sat for nearly a hundred years was in the room that used to be their bedroom. I wanted to get it refinished properly before using it again, but hadn't been able to afford it yet. With a piece that old, it was also a pain to find anyone willing to work on it.

"Where are you going?"

"I just want to check something."

The desk had been built for a typewriter to be hidden within. When the top was closed, it looked like a normal desk. Nothing special about it.

I pulled at the drawers. The sight of every empty space filled me with disappointment. What was I doing wrong? Why couldn't I find it?

"May I?"

I motioned Eirene forward and she felt around, pressing seemingly at random until a drawer popped open. An envelope had been stuffed inside. It had yellowed with age and the glue had long since dried out, so it opened easily.

*Dear Lenore,*

*I hope that I have told you about the type-writer before this point, but I doubt I'll have the chance. You're still so young, so it is my wish that this letter will suffice and you will find it when you need it. You come from a long line of story-*

*tellers. The words you write are your legacy and I hope that you'll find that the typewriter I gifted you helps you bring the words to life...*

I BLINKED as I read the rest of the letter silently, mouthing the words as I went.

"You are descended from a Traveller," the letter said. Traveller, with a capital T. What was a Traveller? It was written like I should know what it meant. My fingers traced the edges of the paper. Perhaps Sean did.

I glanced back towards the other room. I didn't want to ask him. Not yet.

Perhaps I wasn't some chosen one, but that didn't matter. Grandpa had known what the typewriter was and he had left it to me.

"I hate to interrupt," Sean said, the sarcasm thick in his voice, "but the sun's set and we're almost out of time."

I glanced up. Outside the window was dark, though that didn't mean much. The sun set behind the buildings across the street. The sunrises from the shop were always beautiful over Little Turtle Lake. The sunsets from my apartment were lovely as well. It felt like you could see for miles with the lake and park near my apartment building. When they glowed bright orange and pink, there was something magical about them.

"I think I know how to fix this."

At least, I hoped I did. The instructions were so simple, beyond simple. But it made sense that just finishing the story wouldn't do anything to undo the spell.

I pulled out my phone and led them back into the other room.

"Can you find some matches?"

Both of them blinked.

"What are matches?" Eirene asked.

Sean's eyes widened. "You're not planning to burn the type-writer, are you?"

I shook my head. "Not the typewriter."

Quickly, I snapped a couple of pictures of the pages that had Eirene, flipping through the binder to be sure I got them all. I wasn't willing to lose all those months of work to send her home.

He frowned as he watched me open the binder rings and pull the pages out.

"Can you find a bowl or a pot or something? Metal or glass. The bigger the better."

Sean nodded sharply, moving into the kitchen to look for something. I knew I left some there for making lunch and what-not. Having a kitchen and an apartment upstairs from your place of work was surprisingly useful. When I first came back, I lived there prior to getting my own place and still used it as my writing studio. The midnight freight trains drove me crazy as they vibrated the whole building and I always wished that my grandfather had built the shop a bit further away from the tracks, but at least he had put the bedroom in the front of the building, facing the road, so there was a bit of buffer between the bedroom and the train tracks.

There was a moment of hesitation. I hadn't copied these pages into the computer yet. Was there enough time to take pictures? It was some of my best work and it would be a shame to lose them.

"What are you doing?" Sean asked as I pulled my phone out and took some quick pictures.

Flipped the page. Snap a picture. Fortunately, the section where Eirene was in wasn't that long.

I ripped the paper into tiny pieces into the bowl that Sean produced before setting it into the metal sink. I struck one of the matches and tossed it in the bowl with the paper.

The flames flared high, unlike on TV, and for a moment, I

wondered if I should have gotten some water or the fire extinguisher to douse it. But the flames leveled out quickly and the paper began to turn brown and crumple into ash.

The letter's instructions were clear.

"Stand over here," I told Eirene, pointing at a clear spot on the floor that would be easy enough to vacuum once she was gone.

After it finished burning, I scattered the ashes in a circle on the floor around her.

"What now?"

I glanced at Sean. "You said that spells are simple. That it's just the intent." I looked at Eirene. "I want you to go home. But do you want to?"

She closed her eyes and let out a breath. "I do. I want to go home."

No sooner had she finished speaking when the ashes began to glow. The floor inside the ring lit up and a tunnel of wind swirled around her. It blew my hair into my face, making me blink against the dust it kicked up. And when the wind stopped, Eirene was gone.

IT WAS strange to think that this afternoon, I hadn't known that magic was real. The only magic I truly believed in before was the magic of creating art.

Inside my apartment, the cat seemed to have made himself at home on my couch. He had curled up and was napping contently. I turned back to Sean, who stood awkwardly in the hallway.

"I'm sorry I couldn't help you."

"I knew it was a long shot." He gave me a wry smile. "But there's always another way."

I nodded. I wouldn't invite him in, not after he had barged his way into my home earlier in the evening. I could practically hear Gia snickering and vowed I'd edit the story when— if I told her.

"Good night, Sean."

Something in his face softened and he bowed his head. "Good night."

I smiled and closed the door behind me, locking it for the night. Part of me wanted to open the door again. To do what... I wasn't sure. But the thought of him walking away now was unbearable. My head rested against the door and I let myself entertain the thought that maybe he was on the other side, doing the same.

When had I ever written about a moody fae, that he was so certain it was me who had brought him here? None of my stories were about condescending, shapeshifting strangers whose moods were impossible to predict.

The clock on the town hall struck and the cat sprang to his feet, eyes wide open. He butted his head against my hand. His time for leaving had passed as well and with the ashes being used to send Eirene back, I didn't know how to go about doing that. The cat didn't seem to mind being here too much though.

"Mrow?"

I scratched between his ears.

The clock continued to chime.

"I guess it's midnight."

He purred loudly.

"You like the name 'Midnight'?"

"Meow," he said in agreement before slipping away from my hand to stretch out along the length of the sofa.

Sean's and Midnight's time for leaving has passed.
What will happen to them?

Find out when their adventures continue in book two of *a Winter Falls Mystery*.

# THE RAVEN PRINCE

❧❧❧

This story is Sean's origin story,<br>
which was written by Lenore when she was<br>
in high school.

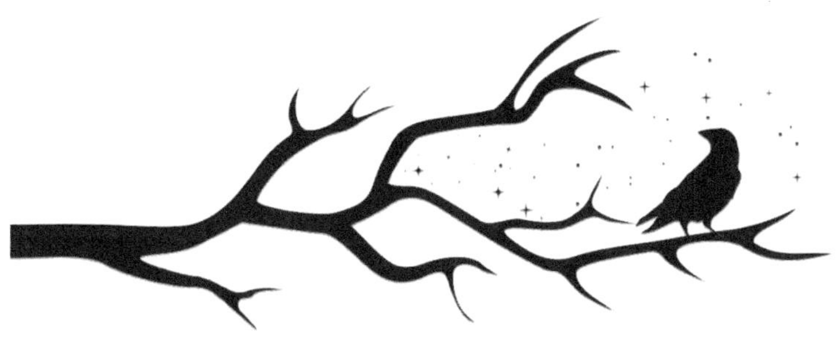

FLOWERS of a thousand shades painted the fields around the castle by the sea. The crisp air brushed against his cheeks and nose, rustled through his hair, and set the flowers swaying like waves across the sapphire sea. In Sean's opinion, this was the most beautiful spot in the whole world.

The world ended at the edges of the island for him. His parents forbid him from traveling across the sea or traveling Beyond. The closest he got to either was wading into the water along the rocky shore or listening to people spin wild tales of the worlds through the rings that took them Beyond. It was just as well. The Beyond held nothing for him.

He was the eldest son of King Fiachra and his queen Órlaith. It made him the second most important person on the isle. Therefore, he had a sacred duty to his people to one day rule them wisely. But he didn't feel ready to be responsible for so many. The closer it came time for him to take the throne, the heavier the crown looked. He didn't think he would ever feel ready to be king.

Tomorrow, he would be confirmed as the crown prince before the Court and then the crown would turn into a noose, slowly strangling the life from him.

Sean sighed as he sat up, running his fingers across the flowers petals. The sun felt good on his skin. The warmth reminded him of spring, despite the brisk air autumn breeze.

He didn't want to go home yet. Lessons would resume and there was a rather large gathering tonight with all of the nobles of the Court. He would be on display at that point for the rest of the evening until everyone went home. It was his least favorite occasions. Being a public figure didn't come as naturally to him as it did the rest of his family.

His older sisters, Fionnuala and Aoife, were better suited to rule. Both were strong and wise. They were accomplished stateswomen in their own right and people respected them. Sean was proud of his sisters, but when he stood next to them, he always felt inadequate and unprepared.

Fionnuala had married into a good family and would have made a good queen. She loved their people in a kind, unselfish sort of way. But so long as Sean was heir, she could never inherit the throne.

*It wasn't fair*, he thought as he watched the wind rippling the flowers. *As the firstborn child, Fionnuala deserved to be queen.*

Aoife's kindness was legendary. She would help anyone in need, but was also a brave warrior. She led trainings and headed the war council, not that they had been at war in quite some time. If they did go to battle, the people would be in good hands under her wise guidance.

All he had was his magic. He would rather spend his time in the tower with the books or sitting by the sea dreaming than he would in a council session. But his father wouldn't listen to reason when it came to such things and neither would the council. The people would accept no other successor, so long as Sean lived.

The sun had long since passed its high point and was sinking fast beyond the clouds and cliffs, sending streaks of dazzling oranges and pinks and purples across the sky. It was late and he should be getting back but he found himself oddly reluctant.

*The long way it is.*

The fields along the sea turned into the woods by a lake. The woods were unfamiliar. Beautiful, but sad. A light lit the way in front of him, dancing between the shadows. The closer he came to it, the further away it moved, leading him deeper and deeper into the woods. The trees thinned and gave way to a clearing.

Instinctually, he knew he should turned back. No good ever came from such magic. And yet...

In the next second, the light came from across the misty lake, where he knew no island had ever been. Sean took a step forward, mindful of the way the murky waters could drop out from beneath one's feet if they weren't careful. When the sea reached his knees, he turned back to the shore but the fog had grown so thick that he couldn't see behind him. Only forward existed, towards that bright light.

A small boat knocked into his legs, bobbing gently on the waves. It was empty and Sean held onto the edges. It took a bit of work, but he managed to get himself into the boat. His boots were sopped and he pulled each off to drain them back into the lake.

The oars' weight was unfamiliar to him. He had seen his people row boats out to sea before, but he had never done that himself. His parents forbid it.

What would they think of him out here? They would be angry and that was what settled his decision to continue forward more than anything. If he went back, his parents would ban him from ever going anywhere again. And if he could leave their home, they would send him with guards to watch his every move. At least, if he continued forward, he would have one last bit of freedom for a bit longer.

Despite the waves, the water was still. Figures danced beneath the surface but he knew better than to reach out and touch. The kinds of creatures that lived in strange lakes were not the ones he wanted to disturb. They might drag him under into the abyss and never allow him to return. At least above the water, he could pretend that going home was still an option. Somehow, in his heart, he knew it wasn't so simple. Not anymore.

The shore on the distant island was different from the rocks he left behind. Grains of soft white sand so fine that it almost looked like snow covered the beaches.

He jumped out onto the beach, his boots leaving deep impressions on the shore.

Everything was strange here. All around him, the air was thick with magic so ancient that it took his breath away. It made his blood sing in his veins and he closed his eyes to fully savor it.

When he opened his eyes, the light flickered before him. It didn't feel dangerous or mischievous or willing to cause him harm. It felt like tit was leading him home.

There was really no choice but to follow it forward.

The light stopped inside a ring, hovering just inside the edge of the circle. He wasn't sure why he felt like he could trust it so fully, but he knew it wouldn't lead him astray.

Something about the ring called him inside.

Like the rings on the mainland, this ring was made of a variety of mushrooms. Some of the rings on the mainland had been there for centuries, perhaps longer. He didn't know where any of them led, but he had heard the Travellers tell stories all the time when he sneaked out. His parents would have frowned if they knew where he went.

Every crown prince before him went out into the world on a journey of discovery. While they weren't at war, the peace his people currently enjoyed was an uneasy one, enough for his parents to worry. As a result, he had never traveled to foreign lands or saw how others lived the way his father had before he prepared to take the throne. Maybe that was why Sean was so unready to take on all of his responsibilities. To be a king, he felt like he needed to be something more.

Perhaps that was why he was so willing to go forward and follow an unknown source of magic. He spent his whole life doing as his parent bade. With the rare and rather minor rebellions, sneaking out to listen to stories and sit in a field with flowers, he had lived for their expectations. The same expectations that he expected to crumble under their immense weight.

He took a step in. Then another. A feeling of deep peace washed over him and Sean closed his eyes, letting the magic embrace him fully. Something tugged at him, a hand on the back of his neck, his elbow, his wrist. It pulled him forward, almost insistently.

Sean gasped sharply and opened his eyes. The light danced before him, bobbing gently in place. It split into a thousand tiny stars, flashing and spinning around him. His stomach twisted uncomfortably, his breath caught in his throat, and before he could think of trying to escape, the floor fell out from under his feet.

# Also by the Author

## Lady Thea's World

An Invitation to Tea: A Historical Romance Novella

• • •

## A Lady Thea Mystery

Book 1: Murder on the Flying Scotsman

Book 1.5: The Unread Letter

Book 2: The Corpse at Ravenholm Castle

Book 3: A Most Fashionable Murder

Book 3.5: A Christmas Puzzle

• • •

## A Prescott House Mystery

## Book 1: Murder at the Midnight Ball

# Acknowledgments

Cover designed by Jessica Baker.

Elements from Canva.com:

Cover:
• Rena Creation
• easyart
• Marina Zlochin
• @tania-chaban
• Sketchify Korea

Chapter Titles and Scene Breaks:
• GDJ from pixabay
• akash kumar khosla
• mingming's Images
• Ouch! Illustrations

## About the Author

Named for the famous fictional mystery writer Jessica Fletcher, Jessica Baker picked up a pen when she was in elementary school and never set it down.

Jessica lives in sunny Central Florida and is a member of the National Sisters in Crime. When she's not writing, she works at a university and freelances as a camera assistant in film which provides plenty of inspiration for her stories.

To learn more about Jessica and her books, visit her at www.jessicabakerauthor.com and for the latest information, subscribe to her newsletters.

9 781960 102058